# THANK YOU, TEACHER!

Written by
**Cate Berry**

Pictures by
**Sara Varon**

**Balzer + Bray**
*An Imprint of HarperCollins Publishers*

Thanks to the following teachers for their great
classroom suggestions and reference photos:

Kate Bailey
Rebecca Boswell
Katy Butler
Jen de Oliveira
Emily Gearhart
Clara Ellertson Lin
Angela Pawola
Sarah Stanitis
Zoey Turek

Balzer + Bray is an imprint of HarperCollins Publishers.

Thank You, Teacher!
Text copyright © 2023 by Cate Berry
Illustrations copyright © 2023 by Sara Varon
All rights reserved. Manufactured in Italy.

Library of Congress Control Number: 2022931782
ISBN 978-0-06-249157-2

The artist used a Pentel brush pen on Bristol paper for the linework and Photoshop
for the coloring to create the illustrations for this book.
Typography by Dana Fritts
22 23 24 25 26   RTLO   10 9 8 7 6 5 4 3 2 1
❖
First Edition

you are the best

For Jane, Cynthia,
Jen, & Adrienne
—C.B.

To teachers (of all kinds)
everywhere
—S.V.

to the
apple of
my eye

thanks for
beeing a
great teacher

**We** can't believe it's really here!
The ending of an awesome year.
We know you'll miss us
(don't cry *too* long).
Now we'll sing our thank-you song.

Thank you for your morning "Howdy!"
even if it ended rowdy.

Thank you for the circle times,
letting me shout all the rhymes!

Thank you for the gentle nudge.

I need a little nudge to budge.

Thanks for letting me hug tighter—
I bet that spider was a biter.

Thanks for reffing when we fight—
you can always make things right.

Thanks for sitting down at lunch,
even if you had to scrunch.

Thanks for all the science stuff.
We love it when the class erupts!

Thanks for helping paste and glue—
I love it when I'm stuck on you.

Thanks for catching Mr. Furr.
We didn't know how fast you were!

that one time I *almost* blew it.

Thanks for sharing that one book.
Who knew *one* book was all it took?

Thanks for staying, hanging in,
all those times from start to end.

The times we raced,

the times we spaced,

the times we shared,

the times we dared,

the times we yowled,

the times we growled,

the times we wiggled,

the times we giggled,

the times we lined up,

the times we . . . didn't.

Thanks for giving all you've got
every time we were . . .

a lot.

new books

Sorry that the summer's here.